IW 14

£1

D1151946

To Louie and Cecil Jarman
for many happy Cumbrian Christmases.
J.J.

For Jack
P.L.

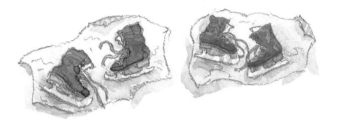

First published in Great Britain 1993
by William Heinemann Ltd and Mammoth
imprints of Reed Consumer Books Ltd
Michelin House, 81 Fulham Road, London SW3 6RB
and Auckland, Melbourne, Singapore and Toronto

Reprinted by Mammoth 1994
0 7497 1624 X

Text copyright © Julia Jarman 1993
Illustrations copyright © Priscilla Lamont 1993

A CIP catalogue record for this title
is available from the British Library
The right of Julia Jarman and Priscilla Lamont
to be identified as author and illustrator of
this work has been asserted by them in accordance
with the Copyright, Designs and Patents Act 1988

Produced by Mandarin Offset
Printed and bound in China

WILL THERE
—— BE ——
POLAR BEARS?

Julia Jarman

illustrated by Priscilla Lamont

MAMMOTH

"We're going away for Christmas
this year," said Sam's mum.
"Away?" said Sam. "Where to?"
"To stay with Great Aunt Addie," said Dad.
"You'll like her, she's fun. She taught me
how to skate."

Sam ran to tell Megan.
"Yes, I know," said Megan.
Megan knew everything.

"Where does Great Aunt Addie
live?" asked Sam.
"Up North," said Megan.

"Is it far?" asked Sam.
"Miles and miles," she said.

"Is it near the North Pole?" Sam asked.
But Megan only laughed.

"Will there be ice and snow and
polar bears? My penguin will like that."
Sam thought about it all.

"I bet Aunt Addie lives in an igloo," he said.
"She'll have a sledge with husky dogs to pull
her along."

She must be a very special aunt. Perhaps that's
why she was called *Great* Aunt.

But later that day, Sam had a worrying thought. "Megan, what about our presents? How will Father Christmas know where to take them?" "Write and tell him," she said. "I'll help."

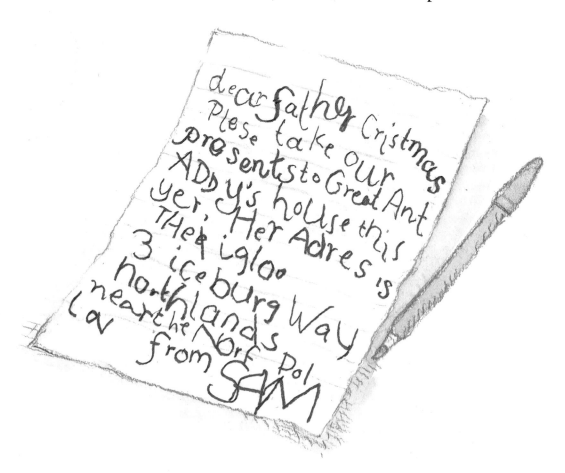

dear father Cristmas
Plese take our Ant
presents to Great Ant
ADDy's house this
yer. Her Adres is
THe igloo
3 iceburg Way
northlands
near the Norf Pol
Lv from Sam

"It'll be nearer for him anyway," said Sam.
"Not so far for the reindeer," said Megan with a smile.
Sam posted his letter. He could hardly wait till Christmas.

But he had to wait, until at last it was Christmas Eve
and time to go.
"Shouldn't we be going by plane,"
he asked, "or boat?"

The journey was long
and Sam slept in the car
till Mum's shout woke him up: "Here we are!"
"But where's the snow?" asked Sam.
"There's some on top of the hills," said Dad.
"And it's icy cold. There'll be more tonight."

When they got to Great Aunt Addie's,
she looked ordinary. She lived in an ordinary house
with an ordinary cat and an ordinary dog called Douglas.

Aunt Addie had tea ready, but Sam couldn't eat
anything. She asked him why he looked so sad.
"I wrote and told Father Christmas that you
lived near the North Pole," he said. "But you
don't and he won't know where to bring my
presents."
Aunt Addie nodded. Then she said: "When I
was a little girl, I used to hang my letter to
Father Christmas on a special tree at the top
of the hill. Let's write him another letter and
take it there. Look, it's snowing again."

When the letter was finished, Aunt Addie took
down a sledge and they set off into the snowy night.

The moon shone
and the snow sparkled,
and as Aunt Addie pulled Sam
up the hill, she taught him a
special rhyme.

And there at last, at the top of the hill was the special tree! Sam tied his letter to a branch and closed his eyes:

"*Special Christmas wishing tree,*
Give Father Christmas this letter from me."

Then he whizzed down the hill on the sledge.

Back at Aunt Addie's house, Sam told his mum and dad about the letter. Then he hung up his stocking and went to bed.

And while he was sleeping Father Christmas *did* come.

In the morning, his stocking was full and there were more presents for everyone round the Christmas tree.

Later, after a huge Christmas dinner, Aunt Addie said: "Let's all go for a walk up the hill."

So up they all went and there at the top,
hanging on the special tree, were two more
parcels, one for Sam and one for Megan.
"Skates!" yelled Sam as he opened his.
"But we don't know how to skate," said Megan.
"I'll teach you," said Aunt Addie.

And she DID.
Sam was delighted.
"You're the greatest,
Great Aunt Addie," he said.
"This is the best Christmas ever."

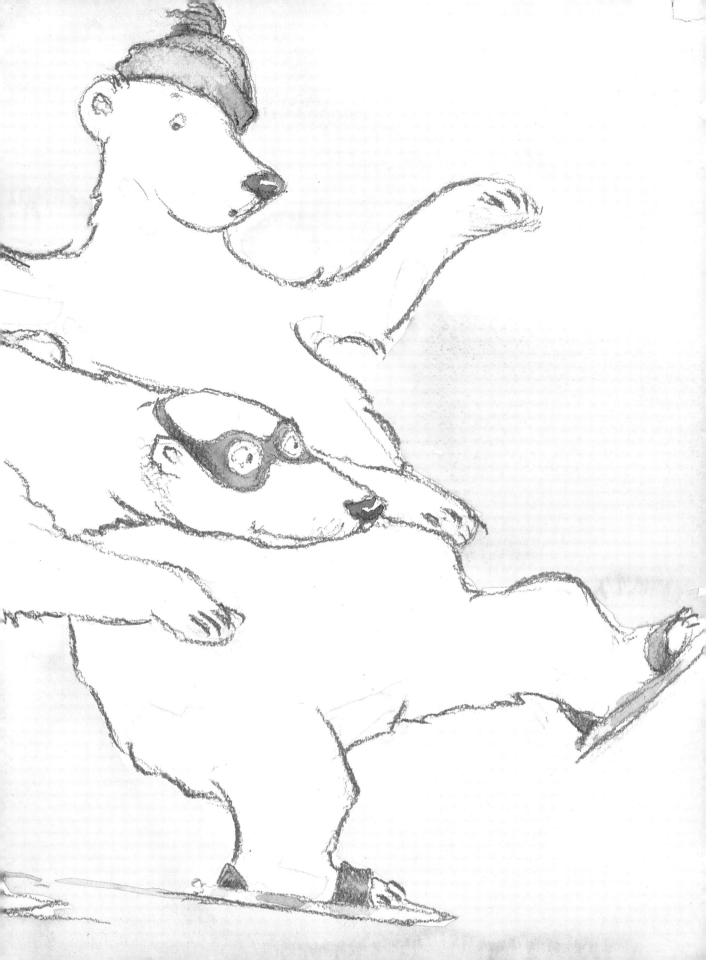